FOREWORD

This novel is now over ninety years old. Yet it remains just as fresh and lively as if it had been written today. The secret of its youth lies in the inspired storytelling of Robert Louis Stevenson, who has created a story with constant appeal to every child's taste for adventure.

Originally published in the magazine Young Folks, Treasure Island *appeared for the first time in book form in 1883, making the young Stevenson famous at the age of thirty-three. Since then, more and more editions have followed, and translations have taken the novel to the eyes of young readers all over the world. Theatrical adaptions and films inspired by Stevenson's work have been numerous, and the interest it has inspired has never dimmed—quite the contrary.* Treasure Island *has become a classic, and one which should be present on every child's bookshelf.*

Published in Great Britain by World Distributors (Manchester) Limited.
P.O. Box 111, 12 Lever Street, Manchester M60 1TS.

Printed in Italy.

SBN 7235 0704 X

Printed in Italy by G. Canale & C. - Torino

ROBERT L. STEVENSON

TREASURE ISLAND

Illustrated by Maraja

WORLD DISTRIBUTORS

The Old Buccaneer

Squire Trelawney and Dr. Livesey having asked me to write down the whole particulars about Treasure Island, keeping back only its bearings, because there is still treasure to be lifted, I go back to the time when my father kept the "Admiral Benbow" inn, and the old seaman first came plodding to our door, his sea-chest following behind him in a hand-barrow.

He was a tall, strong, nut-brown man; his hands ragged and scarred; and a sabre cut across one cheek, a dirty, livid white. He rapped on the door, and called roughly for a glass of rum.

"This is a handy cove," says he; "and a pleasant sittyated grog-shop. This is the berth for me. I'm a plain man; rum and bacon and eggs is what I want. You mought call me captain."

He threw down three or four gold pieces. "You can tell me when I've worked through that," says he.

Each day he would hang about the cove, or upon the cliffs, with a brass telescope; all evening he would sit in the parlour and drink rum and water very strong. Every day he would ask if any seafaring men had gone by along the road, and we saw that he was desirous to avoid them. He promised me a silver fourpenny on the first of every month if I would only keep my "weather-eye open for a seafaring man with one leg".

Some nights, when he had taken a great deal of rum and water, he would sit and sing his wicked old wild sea-songs, and tell dreadful stories about walking the plank, and storms at sea, and wild deeds on the Spanish Main.

He kept on staying week after week, so that all the money had been long exhausted, and still my father never plucked up the heart to insist on having more.

He was only once crossed, towards the end, when my poor father was very ill, and Dr. Livesey came to see the patient.

In the parlour, the captain began to pipe up his eternal song:

> *"Fifteen men on the dead man's chest—*
> *Yo-ho-ho, and a bottle of rum!"*

At last he flapped his hand on the table in a way we all knew to mean—silence. But Dr. Livesey's voice went on as before, speaking clear and kind.

The captain broke out with a villainous, low oath: "Silence, there, between decks!"

"I have only one thing to say to you, sir," replies the doctor, "that if you keep on drinking rum, the world will soon be quit of a very dirty scoundrel!"

The old fellow's fury was awful. He sprang to his feet, drew a sailor's clasp-knife, and threatened to pin the doctor to the wall.

The doctor spoke to him, as before, perfectly calm and steady: "If you do not put that knife this instant in your pocket, I promise that you shall hang at the next assizes."

Then followed a battle of looks between them, but the captain soon knuckled under, put up his weapon, and resumed his seat, grumbling like a beaten dog.

Not long after this, one January morning as I was laying the breakfast table, the parlour door opened and a stranger stepped in. He was a pale, tallowy creature, with a smack of the sea about him.

"Is this here table for my mate Bill?" he asked with a kind of leer. "My mate Bill would be called the captain."

I told him he was out walking, and how soon he was likely to return, and the stranger kept hanging about at the inn door, like a cat waiting for a mouse.

"Here is my mate Bill," he said at last. "You and me'll give Bill a little surprise, bless his 'art."

I was very alarmed as he cleared the hilt of his cutlass and loosened the blade in the sheath. In strode the captain for his breakfast.

"Bill," said the stranger.

The captain spun round on his heel with the look of a man who sees a ghost, or something worse.

"Black Dog!" said he.

"Black Dog as ever was," returned the other. "Come for to see his old shipmate Billy. I'll have a glass of rum from this dear child here, and we'll sit down, and talk square, like old shipmates."

Black Dog sat next to the door, with one eye on his old shipmate, and one, I thought, on his retreat. He bade me go, and for a long time I could hear nothing, until the voices grew higher, and I could pick out a word or two, mostly oaths, from the captain.

"No, no, no, no; and an end of it!" he cried once. "If it comes to swinging, swing all, say I."

Then all of a sudden the chair and table went over in a lump, a clash of steel followed, and then a cry of pain, and the next instant I saw Black Dog in full flight, and the captain hotly pursuing, both with drawn cutlasses, and the former streaming blood from the left shoulder.

Once out upon the road, Black Dog, in spite of his wound, showed a wonderful clean pair of heels, and disappeared over the edge of the hill in half a minute.

The captain, for his part, stood staring like a bewildered man, and at last turned back into the house.

"Jim," says he, "rum. I must get away from here. Rum! Rum!"

I ran to fetch it, but then I heard a loud fall in the parlour, and running in, beheld the captain lying full length upon the floor. My mother came running to help me, and between us we raised his head.

It was a happy relief for us when the door opened and Dr. Livesey came in.

"Oh, doctor," we cried. "Where is he wounded?"

"Wounded? A fiddle-stick's end!" said the doctor. "The man has had a stroke, as I warned him. Now I must do my best to save his trebly worthless life."

The doctor ripped up the captain's sleeve, and exposed his great sinewy arm, which was tattooed with "Here's luck", "A fair wind", "Billy Bones his fancy", and a sketch of a gallows and a man hanging from it.

The doctor took his lancet and opened a vein. A great deal of blood was taken before the captain opened his eyes, and cried: "Where's Black Dog?"

"There is no Black Dog here," said the doctor. "Now, Mr. Bones—"

"That's not my name," he interrupted.

"Much I care," replied the doctor. "What I have to say to you is this: the name of rum for you is death."

About noon I stopped at the captain's door with some medicines, and he seemed both weak and excited.

"Now, matey," said he. "Did that doctor say how long I was to lie here in this old berth?"

"A week at least," said I.

"Thunder!" he cried. "A week! I can't do that: they'd have the black spot on me by then. That Black Dog's a bad 'un, but there's worse that put him on. Now, if I can't get away nohow, it's my old sea-chest they're after. You get on a horse, and go to that eternal doctor swab, and tell him to pipe all hands—magistrates and sich—and he'll lay 'em aboard at the "Admiral Benbow"—all old Flint's crew, all on 'em that's left. I was first mate, and I'm the on'y one as knows the place. But you won't peach unless they get the black spot on me, Jim."

"But what is the black spot, captain?" I asked.

"That's a summons, mate. I'll tell you if they get that."

Probably I should have told the whole story to the doctor; but as things fell out, my poor father died quite suddenly that evening, which put all other matters on one side.

The day after the funeral, I was standing at the door for a moment, full of sad thoughts about my father, when I saw someone drawing slowly near along the road. He was plainly blind, for he tapped before him with a stick, and wore a great green shade over his eyes and nose; and he was hunched, with age or weakness, and wore a huge old tattered sea-cloak with a hood. I never in my life saw a more dreadful-looking figure.

On the floor was a little round piece of paper, blackened on one side. It was the *black spot*. On the other side, I found written: "You have till ten to-night."

I tore open the captain's shirt at the neck, and there, hanging to a tarry string, we found the key to his sea-chest.

A strong smell of tobacco and tar rose up from the miscellany inside. At the bottom there lay a bundle tied up in oil cloth, and a canvas bag that gave forth the jingle of gold. When we were counting our dues, I suddenly heard the tap-tapping of the blind man's stick on the inn door, and the bolt rattling as the wretched being tried to enter. At last, to our joy, the tapping died slowly away.

"I'll take this to square the account," said I, picking up the oilskin packet, as my mother jumped to her feet.

We were less than half way back to the hamlet when our enemies began to arrive, running hard.

There was a pause, then a shout: "Bill's dead, Pew! The money's here, but we don't see Flint's fist nohow."

"Rout the house!" cried Pew. "If you've the pluck of a weevil in a biscuit you'll find them still."

Then from the top of the hill came the tramp of horses galloping. The buccaneers ran, deserting Pew, who turned with a scream, utterly bewildered, and ran right under the first horse.

The riders were revenue officers, led by Supervisor Dance, who had heard news of the lugger in Kitt's Hole. They rode on, but when they reached Kitt's Hole the lugger was already under way.

I went back with Mr. Dance to the inn, and you never

"Will any kind friend inform a blind man where he may now be?" he said.

"You are at the "Admiral Benbow" inn." said I.

I held out my hand, and the horrible eyeless creature gripped it like a vice. "Now, boy," he said, "take me in to the captain."

I obeyed at once, walking towards the parlour, where our sick old buccaneer was sitting, dazed with rum, his cutlass drawn. I saw the blind man pass something into the captain's palm. "Now that's done," he said, tap-tapping back into the road.

The captain looked sharply into his palm. "Ten o'clock!" he cried, and he sprang to his feet.

Even as he did so, he reeled, and then, with a peculiar sound, fell face-foremost to the floor. The captain had been struck dead by thundering apoplexy.

My mother and I were in a very dangerous position, yet we knew that some of the man's money was certainly due to us. At last we went forth together to seek help in the neighbouring hamlet. But no soul would consent to return with us to the inn. The name of Captain Flint carried a great weight of terror.

"Jim and I will have that chest open," said my mother.

We set forth in the cold night, and slipped along the hedges, until we stood alone in the inn with the captain's body.

saw a house in such a state of smash.

"I'll take you along to Dr. Livesey's," said Mr. Dance.

We were told by Dr. Livesey's maid that the doctor was dining with the Squire, and so we walked the short distance to the Hall.

The Squire was a tall man, over six feet high, and broad in proportion, and he had a bluff, rough-and-ready face, all roughened and reddened in his long travels.

The supervisor told his story like a lesson, and you should have seen how the two gentlemen looked at each other in their interest.

"Mr. Dance," said the squire, "you are a very noble fellow. And as for riding down that black, atrocious miscreant, I regard it as an act of virtue, sir, like stamping on a cockroach."

"And so, Jim," said the doctor, "you have the thing that they were after, have you?"

"Here it is, sir," said I, and gave him the packet.

The doctor looked it all over, as if his fingers were itching to open it; but, instead of doing that, he put it quietly in the pocket of his coat. Mr. Dance was further complimented, and at last dismissed.

"And now, squire," said the doctor. "You have heard of this Flint, I suppose?"

"Heard of him!" cried the squire. "He was the blood-thirstiest buccaneer that sailed."

"Supposing that I have here in my pocket some clue to where Flint buried his treasure, will that treasure amount to much?"

"Amount, sir!" cried the squire. "It will amount to this: if we have the clue you talk about, I fit out a ship in Bristol dock, and take you and Hawkins here along, and I'll have that treasure if I search a year."

"Very well," said the doctor. "Now, then, if Jim is agreeable, we'll open the packet."

The bundle was sewn together, and the doctor had to cut the stitches with his medical scissors. It contained two things—a book and a sealed paper.

On the first page of the book there were only some scraps of writing. One was the same as the tattoo mark, "Billy Bones his fancy"; then there were some other snatches, and "Off Palm Key he got itt". I wondered who it was that had "got itt", and what "itt" was that he got. A knife in his back as like as not.

Next came a curious series of entries, with a date at one end of the line and at the other a sum of money. At the end a grand total had been made out, and these words appended, "Bones, his pile".

"The thing is as clear as noonday," cried the squire. "This is the black-hearted hound's account book, with the names of ships or towns that they sank or plundered."

Then the doctor opened the seals on the paper, and there fell out the map of an island. It was about nine miles long and five across, shaped, you might say, like a fat dragon standing up, with a hill in the centre part marked "The Spy-glass". There were crosses of red ink, two on the north part of the island, one in the south-west, and, beside this last, these words, "Bulk of treasure here".

"Livesey," said the squire, "to-morrow I start for Bristol. In ten days' time we'll have the best ship, sir, in England. Hawkins shall come as cabin boy. You, Livesey, are ship's doctor; I am admiral. We'll have favourable winds, a quick passage, and money to eat—to roll in—to play duck-and-drake with ever after."

The Sea Cook

While the squire was hard at work at Bristol, I lived on at the Hall under the charge of old Redruth, the gamekeeper.

One fine day there came a letter from the squire:

"Old Anchor Inn, Bristol, 1, 17–.

Dear Livesey,

The ship is bought and fitted. She lies at anchor, ready for sea. You never imagined a sweeter schooner—a child might sail her—two hundred tons; name, Hispaniola.

The most remarkable stroke of fortune brought me the very man to help me find a crew. I was standing on the dock when I fell in talk with an old sailor who keeps a public house and knows all the seafaring men in Bristol. He has lost his health ashore, and wants a good berth as cook to get to sea again. I engaged him on the spot to be ship's cook. Long John Silver, he is called, and has lost a leg in his country's service. He has no pension, Livesey. Imagine the abominable age we live in!

Silver and myself got together a company of the toughest old salts imaginable—not pretty to look at, but fellows of the most indomitable spirit.

Seaward ho!

JOHN TRELAWNEY."

The next morning, Redruth and I set out for the "Admiral Benbow". The squire had had everything repaired, and I found my mother in good spirits.

The next night, the mail picked us up at the "Royal George" on the heath. I must have dozed a great deal, for when I awakened we were standing in a city street.

"Where are we?" I asked.

"Bristol," said Tom. "Get down."

Our way, to my great delight, lay along the quays and beside the great multitude of ships of all rigs and nations. Then we came in front of a large inn, and met Squire Trelawney, all dressed out like a sea-officer.

"Here you are," he cried, "and the doctor came last night. Bravo! the ship's company complete! We sail tomorrow!"

When I had breakfasted, the squire gave me a note addressed to John Silver, at the sign of the "Spyglass".

The customers were seafaring men; and they talked so loudly that I hung at the door, almost afraid to enter.

As I was waiting, a man came out of a side room, and I was sure he must be Long John. Under the left shoulder he carried a crutch, which he managed with wonderful dexterity. He was very tall and strong, with a face as big as a ham—plain and pale, but intelligent and smiling.

To tell the truth, from the very first mention of Long John I had a fear that he might prove to be the very one-legged sailor whom I had watched for at the inn. But one look at the man before me was enough. I thought I knew what a buccaneer was like—a very different creature, according to me, from this pleasant-tempered landlord.

"Mr. Silver, sir?" I asked, holding out the note.

Just then one of the customers rose suddenly and made for the door, and I recognised him at once.

"Oh," I cried, "stop him! It's Black Dog!"

"I don't care two coppers who he is," cried Silver. "He hasn't paid his score. Harry, run and catch him."

"Has Mr. Trelawney not told you of the buccaneers?" I asked. "He was one of them."

"One of those swabs, was he?" cried Silver. "Ben, run and help Harry. Let's see—Black Dog? No, I don't know the name, not I. Yet I kind of think I've seen the swab. He used to come in here with a blind beggar, he used."

"That was Pew, you may be sure," said I.

My suspicions had been thoroughly reawakened on finding Black Dog at the "Spy-glass", and I watched the cook narrowly. But he was too clever for me, and by the time the two men had come back, and confessed that they had lost the track in a crowd, I would have gone bail for the innocence of Long John Silver.

"I'll step along of you to Cap'n Trelawney and report this here affair," he said.

On our little walk along the quays he made himself the most interesting companion, telling me about the different ships that we passed by.

The squire and Dr. Livesey regretted that Black Dog had got away; but we all agreed that there was nothing to be done, and after he had been complimented, Long John took up his crutch and departed.

"All hands aboard by four this afternoon," shouted the squire after him.

The *Hispaniola* lay some way out, and we went under the figureheads of many other ships, until we got alongside, and were saluted as we stepped aboard by the mate, Mr. Arrow, a brown old sailor, with ear-rings in his ears and a squint. He and the squire were very thick and friendly, but I soon observed that things were not the same between Mr. Trelawney and the captain.

This last was a sharp-looking man, who seemed angry with everything on board, and was soon to tell us why.

"Better speak plain, sir," said the captain to the squire. "I don't like this cruise, and I don't like the men. That's short and sweet. I was engaged, sir, on what we call sealed orders, but now I find that every man before the mast knows more than I do. Next, I learn that we are going after treasure. Now, I don't like treasure voyages on any account; and I don't like them, above all, when the secret has been told to the parrot."

"Silver's parrot?" asked the squire.

"It's a way of speaking," said the captain. "Blabbed I mean."

"Are the crew not good seamen?" asked Dr. Livesey.

"I don't like them, sir," returned Captain Smollett. "I think I should have had the choosing of my own hands."

"The slight, if there be one, was unintentional," said the doctor. "And you don't like Mr. Arrow?"

"I believe he's a good seaman, sir; but he's too free with the crew to be a good officer. A mate shouldn't drink with the men before the mast!"

"Well now," said the doctor. "Tell us what you want."

"Very good," said the captain. "They are putting the powder and the arms in the fore hold. Now, you have a good place under the cabin; why not put them there? Then you are bringing four of your own people with you. Why not give them berths here beside the cabin?"

"I see," said the doctor. "You wish us to keep this matter dark, and to make a garrison of the stern part of the ship, manned with my friend's own people, and

provided with all the arms and powder on board. In other words, you fear a mutiny."

"Sir," said Captain Smollett, "no captain would be justified in going to sea at all if he had ground enough to say that. But I am responsible for the ship's safety and the life of every man-Jack aboard of her. I see things going not quite right."

"I will do as you desire," cried the squire, "but I think the worse of you."

"That's as you please, sir," said the captain. "You'll find I do my duty."

All the night we were in a great hustle, getting things stowed in their place. I was dog-tired when, a little before dawn, the boatswain sounded his pipe, and the crew began to man the capstan-bars. I might have been twice as weary, yet I would not have left the deck; all was so new and interesting to me—the brief commands, the shrill note of the whistle, the men bustling to their places in the glimmer of the ship's lanterns.

Before I could lie down to snatch an hour of slumber the *Hispaniola* had begun her voyage to the Isle of Treasure.

Mr. Arrow turned out even worse than the captain had feared. He had no command among the men, and after a day or two at sea he began to appear on deck with hazy eye, stuttering tongue, and other marks of drunkenness.

We could never make out where he got the drink. But nobody was much surprised when one dark night he disappeared entirely and was seen no more.

"Overboard!" said the captain. "Well, gentlemen, that saves the trouble of putting him in irons."

The boatswain, Job Anderson, then served as mate, and we had a good coxswain in Israel Hands, a wily, old, experienced seaman.

Aboard ship, our cook, Barbecue, as he was known by the men, carried his crutch by a lanyard round his neck, to have both hands as free as possible.

To me he was unweariedly kind; and always glad to see me in the galley, which he kept as clean as a new pin; his parrot in a cage in one corner.

"Here's Cap'n Flint," he would say. "I calls my parrot Cap'n Flint after the famous buccaneer."

And the parrot would say, with great rapidity, "Pieces of eight! pieces of eight! pieces of eight!" till you wondered that it was not out of breath.

"Ah, she's a handsome craft, she is," the cook would say, and the bird would peck at the bars and swear straight on, passing belief for wickedness. "There," John would add, "you can't touch pitch and not be mucked, lad. Here's this poor old innocent bird o' mine swearing blue fire, and none the wiser, you may lay to that."

"Stand by to go about," the parrot would scream.

In the meantime, the squire and Captain Smollett were still on pretty distant terms. "A trifle more of that man," the squire would say, "and I should explode."

It was on the last day of our outward voyage, and I was on my way to my berth, when I thought that I should like an apple. I got bodily into the apple barrel, but what with the rocking movement of the ship, I had fallen asleep, when a heavy man sat down with rather a clash close by, and began to speak. It was Silver's voice, and, before I had heard a dozen words, I understood that the lives of all the honest men aboard depended upon me.

"No, not I," said Silver. "Flint was cap'n; I was quartermaster. I've seen the old *Walrus*, Flint's ship, a-muck with the red blood and fit to sink with gold. I sailed first with England, then with Flint; and I laid by nine hundred safe, from England, and two thousand after Flint. Where's all Flint's men now? Why, most on 'em aboard here."

Long John ran on, little supposing he was overheard.

"Gentlemen of fortune lives rough, and they risk swinging, but when a cruise is done, why, it's hundreds of pounds instead of hundreds of farthings in their pockets. Now, where might you suppose my money was?"

"In Bristol, in banks," answered his companion.

"It were," said the cook, "but my old missus has it all by now, and the old girl's off to meet me."

By this time I had begun to understand that by a "gentleman of fortune" they plainly meant neither more nor less than a common pirate, and the little scene that I had overheard was the last act in the corruption of one of the honest hands.

"Dick's square," said Silver.

"Oh, I know'd Dick was square," returned the voice of the coxswain, Israel Hands. "But, look here, Barbecue: how long are we a-going to stand off and on like a blessed bumboat? I've had a 'most enough o' Cap'n Smollett!"

"Israel," said Silver, "your head ain't much account, nor ever was. Here's a first-rate seaman, Cap'n Smollett, sails the blessed ship for us. If I was sure of you all, I'd have Cap'n Smollett navigate us half-way back again before I struck."

"Why, we're all seamen aboard here," said Dick.

"We're all foc's'le hands," snapped Silver. "We can steer a course, but who's to set one? How many tall ships, think ye now, have I seen laid aboard, and how many brisk lads drying in the sun at Execution Dock? And all for this same hurry and hurry and hurry."

"But," asked Dick, "when we do lay 'em athwart, what are we to do with 'em, anyhow?"

"Well, what would you think?" said the cook. "Put 'em ashore like maroons? Or cut 'em down like that much pork?"

"Billy was the man for that," said Israel. "'Dead men don't bite,' says he."

"I give my vote—death," Silver continued. "When I'm in Parlyment, and riding in my coach, I don't want none of these sea-lawyers in the cabin a-coming home, unlooked for. Dick!" he added, breaking off, "you just jump up and get me an apple, to wet my pipe like."

You may fancy the terror I was in! I heard Dick begin to rise, but then Hands exclaimed: "Oh stow that, John! Let's have a go of the rum."

"Dick," said Silver, "I trust you. I've a gauge on the keg, mind. There's the key; you fill a pannikin."

This must have been how Mr. Arrow got the strong waters that destroyed him, I thought.

Dick was gone but a little while, yet during his absence I gathered some important news; for this whole clause was audible: "Not another man of them'll jine." Hence there were still faithful men on board.

Just then the look-out shouted: "Land ho!"

There was a great rush of feet across the deck, and, slipping in an instant outside my barrel, I dived behind the fore-sail, made a double towards the stern, and came out upon the open deck.

Away to the south-west of us we saw two low hills, and rising behind one of them a third and higher hill, whose peak was buried in fog.

The *Hispaniola* was laid a couple of points nearer the wind, a course that would clear the island on the east.

"And now, men," said the captain, when all was sheeted home, "has any one of you ever seen that land ahead?"

"I have, sir," said Silver. "I've watered there with a trader I was cook in."

"The anchorage is on the south, behind an islet, I fancy?" asked the captain.

"Yes, sir; Skeleton Island they calls it. It were a main place for pirates once."

"I have a chart here," says Captain Smollett. "See if that's the place."

Long John's eyes burned in his head as he took the chart; but I knew he was doomed to disappointment. This was not the map from Billy Bones's chest, but a copy, complete in all things, except for the red crosses and written notes. Sharp as must have been his annoyance, Silver had the strength of mind to hide it.

"Yes, sir," said he, "this is the spot, to be sure."

Just then Dr. Livesey called me to his side, and asked me to fetch his pipe. But I broke out immediately:

"Doctor, let me speak. I have terrible news."

The doctor changed countenance a little, but next moment he was master of himself; and the next thing I heard was the captain giving an order, and all hands were piped on deck and served with double grog.

The three gentlemen went below, and word was sent forward that Jim Hawkins was wanted in the cabin.

"Now, Hawkins," said the squire. "Speak up."

I told the whole details of Silver's conversation.

"Captain," said the squire, "you were right, and I was wrong. I own myself an ass, and I await your orders."

"No more an ass than I, sir," returned the captain. "I never heard of a crew that meant to mutiny but what showed signs before. But this crew beats me."

"Captain," said the doctor, "with your permission, that's Silver. A very remarkable man."

"He'd look remarkably well from a yard-arm, sir," returned the captain. "Now then, first point; we must go on, because if I gave the word to go about they would rise at once. Second point: we have time before us—at least, until this treasure's found. Third point: there are faithful hands."

"And to think that they're all Englishmen!" broke out the squire.

"Well, gentlemen," said the captain, "we must lay-to, and keep a bright look-out, till we know our men."

"Jim here can help us," said the doctor. "The men are not shy with him, and he is a noticing lad."

"Hawkins, I put prodigious faith in you," added the squire.

My Shore Adventure

When I came on deck next morning, we were lying becalmed about half a mile to the south-east of the low eastern coast.

The *Hispaniola* was rolling scuppers under in the ocean swell, and creaking, groaning, and jumping like a manufactory. My heart sank into my boots; and from that first look onward I hated the very thought of Treasure Island.

All the way in, Long John stood by the steersman and conned the ship, for he knew the passage like the palm of his hand.

The men lay about the deck growling together in talk. Mutiny, it was plain, hung over us like a thundercloud.

We held a council in the cabin.

"Sir," said the captain, "if I risk another order, the whole ship'll come about our ears by the run. Now, Silver is anxious as you and I to smother things up. Let's allow the men an afternoon ashore. Silver'll bring 'em aboard again as mild as lambs."

It was so decided; loaded pistols were served out to all the sure men; and the captain went on deck and gave the news.

Then it was that there came into my head the first of the mad notions that contributed so much to save our lives. It occurred to me at once to go ashore. In a jiffy I had curled up in the fore-sheets of the nearest boat.

The boat I was in shot far ahead of her consort, and the bow had struck among the shore-side trees, and I had plunged into the nearest thicket, while Silver and the rest were still a hundred yards behind.

All at once a wild duck flew up with a quack and I judged at once that some of my shipmates must be drawing near.

I crawled under cover of the nearest thicket, and squatted there, hearkening to these desperadoes. In a little green dell beside the marsh, Long John Silver and another of the crew stood in conversation.

"It's because I thinks gold dust of you," Long John was saying. "It's to save your neck that I'm a-speaking."

"Silver," said the other man, "you're old, and you're honest, or has the name for it; and you're brave, or I'm mistook. And will you tell me you'll let yourself be led away by that kind of a mess of swabs? If I turn agin in my dooty—"

I had found one of the honest hands—and here, at that same moment, came news of another. Far away out in the marsh there arose a sound like a cry of anger, then one horrid, long-drawn scream.

Tom leaped at the sound, but Silver did not wink an eye.

"In heaven's name," said Tom, "what was that?"

"That?" returned Silver, smiling away. "Oh, I reckon that'd be Alan."

"Alan!" cried poor Tom like a hero. "Then rest his soul for a true seaman! You've killed Alan, have you? Kill me, too, if you can. If I die like a dog, I'll die in my dooty."

And with that this brave fellow set off walking for the beach. With a cry, John seized the branch of a tree, whipping the crutch out of his arm-pit, and sent that uncouth missile hurtling through the air. It struck poor Tom with stunning violence, in the middle of his back. His hands flew up, he gave a gasp, and fell.

I ran as I never ran before, fear growing upon me until

it turned into a kind of frenzy.

Suddenly I saw a figure leap behind the trunk of a tree. It seemed dark and shaggy; more I knew not, and I began to recall what I had heard of cannibals.

Suddenly, the recollection of my pistol flashed into my mind, and with courage in my heart I walked forward.

"Who are you?" I asked.

"Ben Gunn," he answered, and his voice sounded hoarse and awkward, like a rusty lock. "I'm poor Ben Gunn, I am; and I haven't spoke with a Christian these three years."

He was clothed with tatters of old sea cloth; held together by brass buttons, and bits of stick.

"Three years!" I cried. "Were you shipwrecked?"

"Nay, mate," said he, "marooned."

I knew that this was a horrible kind of punishment in which the offender is left behind on some desolate island.

"I've lived on goats since then, and berries, and oysters," he continued. "You wouldn't happen to have a piece of cheese about you now? No? Now you, what do you call yourself, mate?"

"Jim," I told him.

"Now, tell me true, Jim—ain't that Flint's ship?"

"No, but there are some of Flint's hands aboard," said I.

"Not a man—with one—leg?" he gasped.

I told him the whole story of our predicament.

"You're all in a clove hitch, ain't you, Jim?" he said. "Well, you just put your trust in Ben Gunn. I were in Flint's ship when he buried the treasure. Well, I was in another ship three years back, and we sighted this island. 'Boys,' says I, 'let's land and find Flint's treasure.' Twelve days they looked for it, until one fine morning, 'Benjamin Gunn,' says they, 'you can stay here and find the treasure for yourself.' And here I am."

"Well," said I, "how am I to get on board?"

"There's my boat," said he. "Under the white rock."

Just then there bellowed the thunder of a cannon.

"They have begun to fight!" I cried. "Follow me."

The Stockade
Narrative continued by the doctor

Waiting on the *Hispaniola* was a strain, and we were alarmed for Jim Hawkins' safety. We talked matters over in the cabin, and it was decided that Hunter and I should go ashore in quest of information.

We pulled straight in, in the direction of the stockade upon the chart.

It was a stout log-house, fit to hold two score people on a pinch, and loopholed for musketry on every side. All round was a wide space, and then a paling six feet high. The people in the log-house might hold the place against a regiment.

Suddenly there came ringing over the island the cry of a man at the point of death. "Jim Hawkins is gone," was my first thought.

I made up my mind instantly, and with no time lost

returned to the shore, and jumped on board the jolly-boat.

By good fortune Hunter pulled a good oar. We made the water fly; and I was soon aboard the schooner.

I found them all shaken, as was natural. The squire was sitting down, as white as a sheet, thinking of the harm he had led us to, the good soul!

I told my plan to the captain, and between us we settled on the details of its accomplishment.

We put old Redruth in the gallery between the cabin and the forecastle, with three or four loaded muskets and a mattress for protection. Joyce and I set to work loading the jolly-boat, with powder tins, muskets, bags of biscuits, kegs of pork, a cask of cognac, and my invaluable medicine chest.

In the meantime the squire and the captain stayed on board, and the latter hailed the coxswain, who was the principal man aboard.

"Mr. Hands," he said, "here are two of us, with a brace of pistols each. If any one of you six make a signal of any description, that man's dead."

They were a good deal taken aback; and, after a little consultation, one and all tumbled down the fore companion, thinking no doubt, to take us on the rear. But when they saw Redruth waiting for them in the sparred gallery, they went about-ship at once, and a head popped out again on deck.

"Down, dog!" cries the captain.

And the head popped back again; and we heard no more, for the time, of these six very faint-hearted seamen.

By this time, we had the jolly-boat loaded, and Joyce and I made for shore again as fast as oars could take us.

Just before we lost sight of the watchers along shore, one of them whipped ashore and disappeared.

All three made the first journey to the block-house, heavily laden with stores. Leaving Joyce to guard them, Hunter and I returned to the jolly-boat, and loaded ourselves once more. So we proceeded, until the whole cargo was bestowed, when the two servants took up their positions in the block-house, and I, with all my power, scuttled back to the *Hispaniola*.

The squire was waiting for me at the stern window, and we fell to loading the boat for our very lives.

Redruth retreated from his place in the gallery, and dropped into the boat, which we then brought round to the ship's counter for Captain Smollett.

"Now, men," said he, addressing the mutinous hands. "Do you hear me? It's to you, Abraham Gray, I am speaking. I am leaving this ship and I order you to follow your captain. I give you thirty seconds to join me in."

There was a pause, then a sudden scuffle, a sound of blows, and out burst Abraham Gray with a knife-cut on the side of the cheek.

"I'm with you, sir," said he.

The little gallipot of a boat that we were in was gravely overloaded, and we were swept by the current out of our true course, and away from the proper landing-place behind the point.

Suddenly the captain cried, "The gun! Look astern!"

We had entirely forgotten the long nine; and there, to our horror, were the five rogues busy about her. It flashed into my mind that the round-shot and the powder for the gun had been left behind.

"Israel was Flint's gunner," said Gray hoarsely.

I could see that brandy-faced rascal, Israel Hands, plumping down a round-shot on the deck.

"Mr. Trelawney, you're the best shot," said the captain. "Will you please pick me off one of those men, sir?"

Hands, who was at the muzzle with the rammer, was the most exposed. But just as Trelawney fired, he stooped, the ball whistled over him, and it was one of the others who fell.

The cry he gave was echoed by a great number of voices from the shore, and I saw the other pirates trooping out from the trees and tumbling into the boats.

We were now close in, but suddenly the boat sank by the stern in three feet of water. We could wade ashore in safety, but there were all our stores at the bottom, and only two guns out of five remained in a state for service.

We made our best speed across the wood, and struck the enclosure on the south side. Almost at the same time, seven mutineers appeared in full cry at the south-western corner. They paused, as if taken aback; and we had time to fire. One of the enemy fell, and the rest plunged into the trees.

But just at that moment a pistol cracked, a ball whistled close past my ear, and poor Tom Redruth stumbled and fell to the ground.

The squire dropped down beside him on his knees and kissed his hand, crying like a child.

"Be I going, doctor?" asked Tom.

"Tom, my man," said I, "you're going home."

The captain climbed on the roof, and with his own hand ran up the British colours; then came forward with another flag and spread it reverently on the body.

Just then, with a roar and a whistle, a round-shot passed high above the roof of the log-house and plumped far beyond us in the wood. All through the evening they kept thundering away, and ball after ball flew over or fell short.

"The ebb has made a good while," observed the captain. "Our stores should be uncovered. Volunteers to go and bring in pork!''

Gray and Hunter stole out of the stockade; but it proved a fruitless mission. For four or five of the mutineers were busy carrying off our stores, and wading out with them to one of the gigs that lay close by.

Suddenly there came a hail on the land side, and I saw Jim Hawkins, safe and sound, come climbing over the stockade.

Narrative resumed by Jim Hawkins

As soon as Ben Gunn saw the colours he came to a halt, stopped me by the arm, and sat down.

"Now,'' said he, "there's your friends. Silver would fly the Jolly Roger, you don't make no doubt of that.''

"Well,'' said I, "that may be so, and so be it; all the more reason that I should hurry on and join my friends.''

"When Ben Gunn is wanted,'' said Ben, "you know where to find him, Jim. Just where you found him today. And him that comes is to have a white thing in his hand: and he's to come alone. Oh, and you'll say this: 'Ben Gunn,' says you, 'has reasons of his own.'''

"Well,'' said I, "I believe I understand. You have something to propose, and you wish to see the squire or the doctor; and you're to be found where I found you.''

"And when? says you,'' he added. "Why, from about noon observation to about six bells.''

"Good,'' said I, "and now may I go?''

"You won't forget?'' he inquired anxiously. "Reasons of his own; that's the mainstay. And, Jim, if you was to see Silver, you wouldn't go for to sell Ben Gunn? Wild horses wouldn't drag it from you? No, says you.''

Here he was interrupted by a loud report, and a cannon-ball came tearing through the trees and pitched in the sand, not a hundred yards away. The next moment each of us had taken to his heels in a different direction.

For a good hour to come, I moved from hiding-place to hiding-place, always pursued, or so it seemed to me, by these terrifying missiles. But towards the end of the bombardment, I had begun to pluck up my heart again; and after a long detour to the east, crept down among the shore-side trees.

The *Hispaniola* still lay where she had anchored; but, sure enough, there was the Jolly Roger—the black flag of piracy—flying from her peak. Even as I looked there came another red flash and another report, and one more round-shot whistled through the air. It was the last of the cannonade.

I lay for some time, watching the bustle which succeeded the attack. Men were demolishing something with axes on the beach near the stockade; the poor jolly-boat, I afterwards discovered. There was a sound in their voices which suggested rum.

At length I thought I might return towards the stockade. As I rose to my feet, I saw an isolated rock pretty high, and peculiarly white in colour. It occurred to me that this might be the very white rock of which Ben Gunn had spoken, and that some day a boat might be wanted, and I should know where to find it.

I skirted among the woods until I regained the stockade, and was welcomed by the faithful party.

I had soon told my story, and began to look about me. The log-house was made of unsquared trunks of pine—roof, walls, and floor. There was a porch at the door, and under this porch a little spring welled up into an artificial basin—no other than a great ship's kettle.

The cold evening breeze whistled through every chink of the rude building, and sprinkled the floor with a continual rain of fine sand. There was sand in our eyes, sand in our teeth, and sand in our suppers.

If we had been allowed to sit idle, we should all have fallen in the blues, but Captain Smollett was never the man for that. All hands were called up before him and he divided us into watches. He then went round from one to another, keeping up our spirits.

"That man Smollett,'' said the doctor, "is a better man than I am.''

Another time the doctor said to me, "You've seen my snuff-box, haven't you, Jim? And you never saw me take snuff; the reason being that in my snuff-box I carry a piece of Parmesan cheese. Well, that's for Ben Gunn!''

Our best hope, it was decided, was to kill off the buccaneers until they either hauled down their flag or ran away with the *Hispaniola*. From nineteen they were already reduced to fifteen; and besides that we had two able allies—rum and the climate.

I was dead tired, and when I got to sleep, I slept like a log of wood. I was awakened by the sound of voices.

"Flag or truce!" I heard someone say; and then, with a cry of surprise, "Silver himself!"

"Who goes?" cried the captain. "Stand or we fire."

"There poor lads have chosen me cap'n, after your desertion, sir," answered Long John. "We're willing to submit, if we can come to terms, and no bones about it. I don't deny that was a pretty good lay of yours last night, Cap'n Smollett. But you mark me, it won't do twice, by thunder! He wasn't dead when I got round to him, not he."

All that Silver said was a riddle to us, but I began to suppose that Ben Gunn had paid the buccaneers a visit.

"We want that treasure, and we'll have it!" said Silver.

"Avast there!" cried Mr. Smollett. "I would see you and this whole island blown clean out of the water into blazes first."

"You give us the chart to get the treasure by," resumed Silver, "and we'll offer you a choice. Either you come aboard along of us, and then I'll give you my affy-davy to clap you somewhere safe ashore. Or, if that ain't to your fancy, you can stay here, and I'll send the first ship I sight to pick you up. Refuse that, and you've seen the last of me but musket-balls."

"Now you'll hear me," said the captain. "If you come up one by one, unarmed, I'll engage to clap you all in irons, and take you home to a fair trial. If you won't, my name is Alexander Smollett, I've flown my sovereign's colours, and I'll see you all to Davy Jones. You can't find the treasure, and you can't sail the ship."

Silver's eyes started in his head with wrath.

"Before an hour's out, I'll stove in your old block-house," he cried, as he stumbled off.

"My lads," said Captain Smollett, "I've given Silver a broadside; and before the hour's out we shall be boarded. We're outnumbered, but we fight in shelter. I've no manner of doubt that we can drub them."

The captain completed the plan of our defences, and ordered us all to our positions. We stood there, each at his post, in a fever of anxiety. An hour passed away.

"Hang them!" said the captain. "This is as dull as the doldrums."

Suddenly, a little cloud of pirates leaped from the woods on the north side. They ran straight on the stockade, and four made good their footing inside our defences. Our position was utterly reversed. Cries and confusion, the flashes and reports of pistol-shots, and one loud groan, rang in my ears.

"Out, lads, out, and fight 'em in the open! Cutlasses!" cried the captain.

I dashed out into the hurly-burly.

Fierce though the fighting was, and long though it lasted, when at last it was over victory was ours. But back in the house I saw at a glance the price we had paid for victory. Hunter lay beside his loophole, stunned; Joyce by his, never to move again; while right in the centre, the squire was supporting the captain.

"Have they run?" asked Mr. Smollett.

"All that could, you may be bound," returned the doctor; "but there's five of them will never run again."

My Sea Adventure

The mutineers had "got their rations for that day", as the captain put it, and we had a quiet time to overhaul the wounded and get dinner.

Out of the eight men who had fallen in the action, only three still breathed—that one of the pirates who had been shot at the loophole, Hunter, and Captain Smollett. Before long the mutineer died of his wounds, and Hunter never recovered consciousness in this world.

As for the Captain, his wounds were grievous, but not dangerous. He was sure to recover, the doctor said, but in the meantime he must not walk or move his arm.

After dinner the squire and the doctor sat by the captain's side a while; and then the doctor took up his hat and pistols, girt on a cutlass, put the chart in his pocket, and with a musket over his shoulder, set off briskly through the trees.

"Why, in the name of Davy Jones," said Gray, "is Dr. Livesey mad?"

"I take it," replied I, "the doctor has his idea; and if I am right, he's going now to see Ben Gunn."

Then I began to get another thought into my head. What I began to do was envy the doctor, walking in the cool shadow of the woods, while I sat grilling, with my clothes stuck to the hot resin, and so much blood about me, and so many dead bodies lying all around.

I was a fool, if you like, and certainly I was going to do a foolish, overbold act; but I was determined to do it. I took a brace of pistols, and as I already had a powder-horn and bullets, I felt myself well supplied with arms.

My scheme was to go down the sandy spit that divides the anchorage on the east from the open sea, find the white rock I had observed last evening, and ascertain whether it was there or not that Ben Gunn had hidden his boat.

I threaded the tall woods, and came forth into the open borders of the grove, and saw the sea lying blue and sunny to the horizon.

Alongside the *Hispaniola* lay one of the gigs, Silver in the sternsheets. All at once there began the most horrid, unearthly screaming, which startled me badly, though I soon remembered the voice of Captain Flint, and even thought I could make out the bird's bright plumage as she sat perched upon her master's wrist.

The white rock was still some eighth of a mile farther down the spit, and it took me a goodish time to get up with it, crawling among the scrub.

Sure enough, there below it was Ben Gunn's boat—home-made if ever anything was home-made: a rude, lopsided framework of tough wood, with a covering of goatskin stretched upon it.

Well, now that I had found the boat, I had taken another notion. This was to slip out under cover of the night, cut the *Hispaniola* adrift, and let her go ashore where she fancied. I had quite made up my mind that the mutineers, after their repulse of the morning, had nothing nearer their hearts than to up anchor and away to sea; this, I thought, would be a good thing to prevent.

It was a night out of ten thousand for my purpose. As the last rays of daylight dwindled and disappeared, absolute blackness settled down on Treasure Island.

I waded through a long belt of swampy sand, and set my coracle, keel downwards, on the surface.

The coracle was both buoyant and clever in a sea-way; but she was the most lopsided craft to manage. She turned in every direction but the one I was bound to go; and I should never have made the ship at all but for the tide. As soon as I was alongside, I laid hold of her hawser.

The hawser was as taut as a bowstring—one cut with my seagully, and she would go humming down the tide.

But it next occurred to me that a taut hawser, suddenly cut, is a thing as dangerous as a kicking horse. Ten to one, if I were to cut it, the coracle would be knocked clean out of the water.

Just then, a light air came, caught the *Hispaniola*, and forced her up into the current; and I felt the hawser slacken in my grasp. I took out my gully, and cut one strand after another, till the vessel only swung by two.

All this time I had heard the sound of loud voices from the cabin. One I recognised for the coxswain's, Israel Hands. The other was a pirate in a red cap, whom I had fought at the stockade. Both men were plainly the worse for drink, and oaths flew like hailstones.

On shore, I could see the glow of the pirates' camp fire, and could hear someone singing:

> *"But one man of her crew alive,*
> *What put to sea with seventy-five."*

At last I felt the hawser slacken once more, and I cut the last fibres through. I was almost instantly swept against the bows of the *Hispaniola*, as she began to turn upon her heel, across the current.

My hands came across a light cord that was trailing overboard across the stern bulwarks. Once I had it in my hands, I pulled in hand over hand on the cord, to have one look through the cabin window.

One glance was sufficient; it showed me Hands and his companion locked together in deadly wrestle, each with a hand on the other's throat.

Just then the whole company on shore broke out into the chorus I had heard so often:

> *"Fifteen men on the dead man's chest—*
> *Yo-ho-ho, and a bottle of rum!*
> *Drink and the devil had done for the rest—*
> *Yo-ho-ho, and a bottle of rum!"*

Suddenly the *Hispaniola* yawed sharply, and I was still being whirled along in her wake. The current had changed at right angles, and there, right behind me, was the glow of the camp fire.

I lay down flat in the bottom of that wretched skiff, and so I must have lain for hours, continually beaten to and fro upon the billows, until at last sleep supervened.

It was broad day when I awoke, and found myself tossing at the south-west end of Treasure Island. I was scarce a quarter of a mile to seaward, and it was my first thought to paddle in and land.

That notion was soon given over. Among the rocks the breakers bellowed; and I saw myself, if I ventured nearer, dashed to death upon the rough shore.

Nor was that all; for crawling together on flat tables of rock, I beheld huge slimy monsters. I have understood since that they were sea-lions and entirely harmless.

But I felt willing rather to starve at sea than to confront such perils, and I preferred to leave Haulbowline Head behind me, and reserve my strength for an attempt to land upon the kindlier-looking Cape of the Woods.

"Well, now," thought I, "I can put the paddle over the side, from time to time, in smooth places."

It was very tiring, and slow work. But suddenly, right in front of me, I beheld the *Hispaniola* under sail.

The beautiful white canvas shone in the sun like snow or silver, and I presumed the men on board were on their way back to the anchorage. Presently she began to fetch more and more to the westward, and at last fell right into the wind's eye, was taken dead aback, and stood there a while helpless, with her sails shivering.

"Clumsy fellows," said I; "they must be drunk as owls."

I set myself to paddle after the unsteered *Hispaniola*. Perhaps I might return the vessel to her captain.

I was now gaining rapidly on the schooner, and, at last, I had my chance. The breeze fell for some seconds, and the *Hispaniola* at last presented me her stern.

And then, of a sudden, I was on the summit of one swell when the schooner came stooping over the next. The bowsprit was over my head. With one hand I caught the jib-boom, and as I clung there panting, the schooner charged down upon the coracle, and I was left, without retreat, on the *Hispaniola*.

I crawled back along the bowsprit, and tumbled on the deck. There was Israel Hands propped against the bulwarks; and the other, red-cap, was on his back.

I observed splashes of dark blood upon the planks, and began to feel sure that they had killed each other in their drunken wrath.

While I was thus looking, Israel Hands turned round, with a low moan, which told of pain and weakness.

"Come aboard, Mr. Hands," I said ironically.

He rolled his eyes round heavily; but all he could do was to utter one word: "Brandy".

In the cabin was such a scene of confusion as you can hardly fancy. All the lockfast doors had been broken open in quest of the chart.

Foraging about, I found a bottle with some brandy left, for Hands; and he must have drunk a gill before he took the bottle from his mouth.

"Ay," said he, "by thunder, but I wanted some o' that!"

"Much hurt?" I asked him.

He grunted, or, rather, I might say, he barked.

"As for that swab," he said, indicating the man with the red cap, "he's good and dead, he is."

"Well," said I, "you'll please regard me as your captain until further notice. By the bye, I can't have these colours; and, by your leave, I'll strike 'em."

Dodging the boom, I ran to the colour lines, handed down their cursed black flag, and chucked it overboard.

"God save the King!" said I, waving my cap; "and there's an end to Captain Silver!"

"Cap'n Hawkins," said Hands at last. "S'pose we talks. Look here, you gives me food and drink; and I'll tell you how to sail the ship; and that's square all round."

In three minutes I had the *Hispaniola* sailing easily before the wind, with good hopes of turning the northern point ere noon, when we might beach her safely.

Hands bound up the great bleeding stab he had received in the thigh, and he began to pick up visibly.

We skimmed before the breeze like a bird.

I was greatly elated with my new command; but the eyes of the coxswain followed me derisively about deck, and there was a shadow of treachery in his expression.

"This here's an unlucky ship, Jim," he said. "There's a sight o' poor seamen been killed in this *Hispaniola*. And now, I'll take it kind if you'd get me a bottle of wine, Jim —this here brandy's too strong for me."

The whole story was a pretext. He wanted me to leave the deck—so much was plain.

"All right," I answered. "I'll bring you port, Mr. Hands. But I'll have to dig for it."

With that I scuttled down the companion with all the noise I could, slipped off my shoes, mounted the forecastle ladder, and popped my head out of the fore companion.

Hands had risen from his position to his hands and knees. In half a minute he had reached the port scuppers, and picked, out of a coil of rope, a long knife, or rather a short dirk, discoloured to the hilt with blood. Hastily concealing it in the bosom of his jacket, he trundled back again into his old place against the bulwark.

It was plain that I was meant to be the victim.

I laid my hand at random on a bottle of wine, and made my reappearance on the deck.

Hands took a good swig of the wine, with his favourite toast of "Here's luck!" Then he lay quiet for a little, and then, pulling out a stick of tobacco, begged me to cut him a quid.

"Cut me a junk o' that," says he, "for I haven't no knife. Cut me a quid, as'll likely be the last, lad; for I'm for my long home and no mistake."

"Well," said I, "if I was you and thought myself so badly, I would go to my prayers, like a Christian man."

"Why?" said he. "Now, you tell me why."

"Why?" I cried. "You've broken your trust; you've lived in sin and lies and blood; there's a man you killed lying at your feet this moment; and you ask me why! For God's mercy, Mr. Hands, that's why."

"For thirty years," he answered, with the most unusual solemnity, "I've sailed the seas, and seen fair weather and foul. Well, now I tell you, I never seen good come o' goodness yet. Him as strikes first is my fancy; dead men don't bite; them's my views."

All told, we had scarce two miles to run. I think I was a good, prompt subaltern, and I am very sure that Hands was an excellent pilot; for we dodged in, shaving the banks, with a certainty and a neatness that were a pleasure to behold.

"Look there," said Hands, "there's a pet bit for to beach a ship in. Starboard a little—so—steady—larboard a little—steady—steady! Now, my hearty, luff!"

The *Hispaniola* ran stem on for the low wooded shore.

The excitement of these last manoeuvres had somewhat interfered with the watch I had kept upon the coxswain. But a sudden disquietude seized upon me, and made me turn my head. There was Hands, with the dirk in his right hand.

He threw himself forward, and I leapt sideways towards the bows. As I did so, I left hold of the tiller, which sprang sharp to leeward. It struck Hands across the chest, and stopped him, for the moment, dead.

Just forward of the main-mast I drew a pistol from my pocket, took a cool aim, and drew the trigger. The hammer fell, but there followed neither flash nor sound; the priming was useless with sea-water. I placed my palms against the main-mast, which was of a goodish bigness, and waited, every nerve upon the stretch.

Seeing that I meant to dodge, he also paused; and a moment or two passed in feints on his part, and corresponding movements upon mine.

Well, while things stood thus, suddenly the *Hispaniola* struck, staggered, ground for an instant in the sand, and then, swift as a blow, canted over to the port side, till the deck stood at an angle of forty-five degrees.

We were both of us capsized in a second, and both of us rolled into the scuppers; the dead red-cap, with his arms still spread out, tumbling stiffly after us. I was the first afoot again. Quick as thought I sprang into the mizzen shrouds, and rattled up hand over hand.

There stood Israel Hands with his face upturned to mine, a perfect statue of surprise and disappointment.

Now that I had a moment to myself, I lost no time in changing the priming of my pistol.

Hands began to see the dice going against him. He also hauled himself heavily into the shrouds and, with the dirk in his teeth, began slowly and painfully to mount. I had quietly finished my arrangements before he was much more than a third of the way up. Then, with a pistol in either hand, I addressed him. "One more step, Mr. Hands," said I, "and I'll blow your brains out! Dead men don't bite, you know," I added with a chuckle.

"Jim," says he, "I reckon we're fouled, you and me, and we'll have to sign articles. I'd have had you but for that there lurch: but I don't have no luck, not I."

I was drinking in his words, as conceited as a cock upon a wall, when, all in a breath, back went his right hand over his shoulder. Something sang like an arrow through the air: I felt a sharp pang, and there I was pinned by my shoulder to the mast. In the horrid pain of the moment, both my pistols went off. With a choked cry, the coxswain plunged head first into the water.

I began to feel sick, faint, and terrified. The dirk, where it had pinned my shoulder to the mast, seemed to burn like a hot iron. I clung with both hands till my nails ached; until I was once more in possession of myself.

The knife, in fact, held me by a mere pinch of skin. I gave a violent shudder, and this tore the skin away, leaving me my own master again.

I went below and did what I could for my wound. I was now alone upon the ship. The jibs I speedily doused and brought tumbling to the deck; but the mainsail was a harder matter. The tide was rapidly fleeting seaward, the schooner settling more and more on her beam-ends.

I waded ashore in great spirits. There lay the schooner, clear at last from buccaneers and ready for our own men to board and get to sea again.

I set my face homeward for the block-house and passed rapidly over my journey, till at last I came to the clearing. There was not a soul stirring, and I began to fear that something had gone wrong.

As I drew nearer, my heart was suddenly and greatly lightened. It is not a pleasant noise in itself, but just then it was like music to hear my friends snoring together so loud and peaceful in their sleep.

In the meantime, there was no doubt of one thing: they kept an infamous bad watch. And then, all of a sudden, a shrill voice broke forth out of the darkness:

"Pieces of eight! pieces of eight! pieces of eight! pieces of eight!" like the clacking of a tiny mill.

Silver's green parrot, Captain Flint! It was she, keeping better watch than any human being, who thus announced my arrival with her wearisome refrain.

At the sharp, clipping tones of the parrot, the sleepers awoke and sprang up; and, with a mighty oath, the voice of Silver cried: "Who goes?"

I turned to run, struck violently against one person, recoiled, and ran full into the arms of a second who, for his part, closed upon and held me tight.

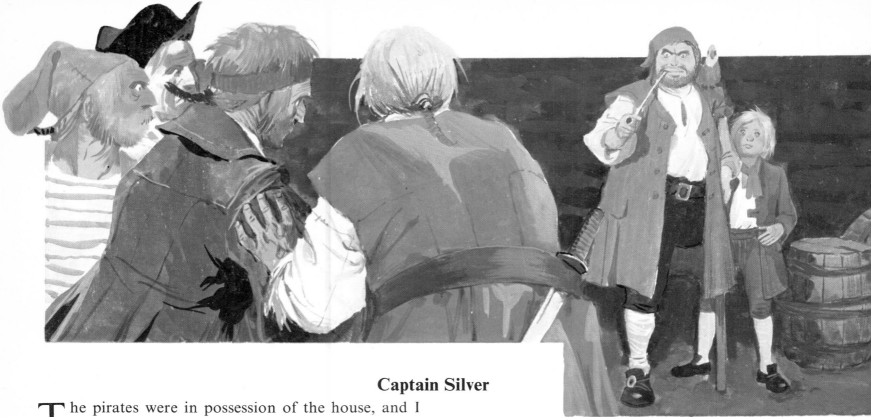

Captain Silver

The pirates were in possession of the house, and I could only judge that all my friends had perished. There were six of the buccaneers, all told; not another man was left alive.

"So," said Silver, "here's Jim Hawkins, shiver my timbers; dropped in, like, eh? Well, come, I take that friendly. I always wanted you to jine and take your share, and now, my cock, you've got to."

My friends, then, were still alive, and though the cabin party were incensed at me for my desertion, I was more relieved than distressed by what I heard.

"Well," says I, growing a bit bolder, "if I am to choose, I declare I have a right to know what's what."

"Yesterday morning," said Silver, "in the dog-watch, down came Dr. Livesey with a flag of truce. Says he: 'Cap'n Silver, you're sold out. Let's bargain.' We bargained, him and I, and here we are. As for them, they've tramped; I don't know where's they are."

"Well," said I, "here you are, in a bad way: ship lost, treasure lost, men lost; and if you want to know who did it—it was I! I no more fear you than I fear a fly."

Silver leant back against the wall, but the crew drew gradually back, and whispered together.

"Pipe up and let me hear it, or lay-to," remarked Silver.

"Ax your pardon, sir," returned one of the men. "This crew's dissatisfied and steps outside for a council."

And with an elaborate sea-salute, he stepped out of the house, the rest following; and left Silver and me alone.

"Now, Jim Hawkins," whispered Silver instantly. "You're within half a plank of death, and they're going to throw me off. Back to back, says I. I'll save your life—if so be as I can—from them. But see here, Jim—tit for tat—you save Long John from swinging."

The door opened, and the five men pushed one of their number forward.

"Step up, lad," cried Silver. "Hand it over, lubber. I know the rules, I do; I won't hurt a depytation."

Thus encouraged, the buccaneer stepped forth more briskly, and passed something to Silver.

"This crew has tipped you the black spot in full council, as in dooty bound," said one of the pirates.

"Thanky, George," replied the sea-cook. "Ah! 'Deposed'—that's it, is it? I'm still your cap'n mind—till you outs with your grievances, and I reply."

"First you've made a hash of this cruise," spoke up one of the men. "Second, you let the enemy out o' this here trap for nothing. Third, you wouldn't let us go at them upon the march. And then, fourth, there's this here boy. We'll all swing and sun-dry for your bungling."

"I made a hash o' this cruise, did I?" said Silver. "Well, now, if you want to know about that boy, why, shiver my timbers, isn't he a hostage? He might be our best chance, and I shouldn't wonder. And number three? Maybe you don't count it nothing to have a real college doctor come to see you every day—you, George Merry, that had the ague-shakes upon you not six hours agone. And as for number two—well, you came crawling on your knees to me to make a bargain—and you'd have starved too, if I hadn't—but that's a trifle! You look here—that's why!"

And he cast down on the floor none other than Billy Bones's chart. Why the doctor had given it to him was more than I could fancy.

The appearance of the chart was incredible to the mutineers. They leapt upon it like cats upon a mouse.

"Mighty pretty," said George. "But how are we to get away with it, and us with no ship?"

"How? Why, how do I know?" said Silver. "Elect whom you please to be your cap'n now, I'm done with it."

"Silver!" they cried. "Barbecue for cap'n!"

I was wakened by a clear, hearty voice hailing us from the margin of the wood:

"Block-house, ahoy!" it cried. "Here's the doctor."

Although I was glad to hear the sound, yet my gladness was not without admixture. I remembered with confusion my insubordinate and stealthy conduct; and I felt ashamed to look him in the face.

"Top o' the morning to you, doctor!" cried Silver. "We've quite a surprise for you, too. We've a little stranger here—he! he! A noo boarder and lodger, sir; slep' right alongside of John—stem to stem we was, all night."

"Not Jim?" said Dr. Livesey.

"The very same Jim as ever was," says Silver.

"Well, well," said the doctor at last, "duty first and pleasure afterwards, as you might have said yourself, Silver. Let us overhaul these patients of yours."

A moment afterwards he had entered the block-house, and with one grim nod to me, proceeded with his work.

"I am mutineers' doctor, or prison doctor, as I prefer to call it," says Doctor Livesey, in his pleasantest way, "and I make it a point of honour not to lose a man for King George (God bless him!) and the gallows."

The rogues looked at each other, but swallowed the home-thrust in silence.

"Well," he added, after he had dosed them round, "now I should like to have a talk with that boy, please."

And he nodded his head in my direction carelessly.

"Then, doctor," said Silver, "you just step outside o' that stockade, and I'll bring the boy down to you."

We advanced across the sand to where the doctor awaited us, and Silver stepped out of earshot.

"So, Jim," said the doctor sadly, "here you are. As you have brewed, so shall you drink, my boy."

I will own that here I began to weep. "Doctor," I said, "you might spare me. I have blamed myself enough; and my life's forfeit anyway. But what I fear is torture. If they came to torture me, I might let slip a word of where the ship is; for I got the ship, and she lies in North Inlet."

"The ship!" exclaimed the doctor.

Rapidly I described my adventures, and he heard me out in silence.

"There is a kind of fate in this," he observed, when I had done. "Every step, it's you that saves our lives; and do you suppose by any chance that we are going to let you lose yours? That would be a poor return, my boy. Silver!" he cried. "Silver! I'll go as far with you as I dare go, and a step beyond," he continued, as the cook drew near again. "If we both get alive out of this wolf-trap, I'll do my best to save you, short of perjury."

Silver's face was radiant. "You couldn't say more, I'm sure, sir, not if you was my mother," he cried.

Dr. Livesey shook hands with me, nodded to Silver, and set off at a brisk pace into the wood.

For my part, I was horribly cast down. Silver, already doubly a traitor, had still a foot in either camp, and there was no doubt he would prefer freedom with the pirates to a bare escape from hanging, which was the best he had to hope on our side.

It was with an uneasy heart that I set forth behind my captors on the quest for treasure.

We made a curious figure, all in soiled sailor clothes, and all but me armed to the teeth. Silver had two guns slung about him, besides the great cutlass at his waist, and a pistol in each pocket. Captain Flint sat perched upon his shoulder and gabbling odds and ends of purposeless sea-talk. I had a line about my waist, and followed after the sea-cook, who held the loose end of the rope.

The other men were variously burthened, with picks and shovels, and food for the midday meal.

We all set out to the beach, where the two gigs awaited us. As we pulled over, there was some discussion on the chart. The terms of the note on the back admitted of some ambiguity. They ran thus:

"Tall tree, Spy-glass Shoulder, bearing a point to the N. of N.N.E.

"Skeleton Island E.S.E. and by E.

"Ten feet."

A tall tree was thus the principal mark. Now, right before us, the anchorage was bounded by a plateau from two to three hundred feet high. The top of the plateau was dotted thickly with pine trees of varying height. Every here and there, one of a different species rose forty or fifty feet clear above its neighbours.

We pulled easily, and, after quite a long passage, landed at the mouth of the second river. Thence we began to ascend the slope towards the plateau.

A heavy-scented broom and many flowering shrubs had almost taken the place of grass. The air was fresh and stirring, and this, under the sheer sunbeams, was a wonderful refreshment to our senses.

The party spread itself abroad, in a fan shape, leaping to and fro. Silver and I followed—I tethered by my rope, he ploughing, with deep pants, among the sliding gravel.

We were approaching the brow of the plateau, when the first man upon the farthest left began to cry aloud in terror.

At the foot of a pretty big pine, and involved in a green creeper a human skeleton lay, with a few shreds of clothing, on the ground. I believe a chill struck for a moment to every heart.

"He was a seaman," said George Merry, who was examining the rags of clothing. "Leastways, this is good seacloth."

"Ay, ay," said Silver, "like enough; you wouldn't look to find a bishop here, I reckon. But what sort of a way is that for bones to lie? 'Taint in natur'."

But for some disarray, the man lay perfectly straight—his feet pointing in one direction, his hands raised above his head, pointing directly in the opposite.

"I've taken a notion into my old numskull," observed Silver. "Here's the compass; there's the tip-top p'int o' Skeleton Island, stickin' out like a tooth. Just take a bearing, will you, along the line of them bones."

It was done. The body pointed straight in the direction of the island, and the compass read duly E.S.E. and by E.

"I thought so," cried the cook; "this here is a p'inter. Right up there is our line for the jolly dollars. This is one of *Flint's* jokes, and no mistake. Him and six men was alone here; he killed 'em, every man."

"If ever sperrit walked, it would be Flint's," said one of the pirates. "'Fifteen Men' were his only song, mates; and I tell you true, I never rightly liked to hear it since."

"Come, come," said Silver, "stow this talk. He's dead, and he don't walk. Fetch ahead for the doubloons."

Partly from the damping influence of this alarm, partly to rest Silver and the sick folk, the whole party sat down as soon as they had gained the brow of the ascent. Silver, as he sat, took certain bearings from the compass.

"There are three 'tall trees'," said he, "about in the

right line from Skeleton Island. 'Spy-glass Shoulder', I take it, means that lower p'int there. It's child's play to find the stuff now. I've half a mind to dine first."

"I don't feel sharp," growled Morgan. "Thinkin' o' Flint—I think it were—as done me."

All of a sudden, out of the middle of the trees in front of us, a thin, high, trembling voice struck up the well-known air:

"Fifteen men on the dead man's chest—
Yo-ho-ho, and a bottle of rum!"

I never have seen men more dreadfully affected than the pirates. The colour went from their six faces by enchantment.

"It's Flint, by—!" cried Merry.

The song had stopped as suddenly as it began.

"Come," said Silver, struggling with his ashen lips to get the word out, "this won't do. This is a rum start: but it's someone skylarking, and you may lay to that."

Already the others had begun to lend an ear to this encouragement, and were coming a little to themselves, when the same voice broke out again, in a faint hail.

"Darby M'Graw," it wailed. "Darby M'Graw! Fetch aft the rum, Darby!"

The buccaneers remained rooted to the ground, their eyes starting from their heads.

"They was his last words," groaned Morgan, "his last words above board."

"Shipmates," cried Silver, "I never was feared of Flint in his life, and, by the Powers, I'll face him dead. There's seven hundred thousand pound not a quarter of a mile from here. When did ever a gentleman o' fortune show his stern to that much dollars?"

"Belay there, John!" said Merry. "Don't you cross a sperrit."

"Sperrit? Well, maybe," said Silver. "But there's one thing not clear to me. There was an echo. Now, no man ever seen a sperrit with a shadow; well, then, what's he doing with an echo to him, I should like to know?"

This argument seemed weak enough to me, but, to my wonder, George Merry was greatly relieved.

"Well, that's so," he said. "'Bout ship, mates! this here crew is on a wrong tack, I do believe. It was like Flint's voice, I grant you, but not just so clear-away like it, after all. It was liker—"

"By the Powers, Ben Gunn!" roared Silver.

"Why, nobody minds Ben Gunn," cried Merry; "dead or alive, nobody minds him."

It was extraordinary how their spirits had returned. Soon they were chatting together, and not long after, hearing no further sound, they shouldered the tools and set forth again.

The first of the tall trees, by the bearing, proved the wrong one. So with the second. The third rose nearly two hundred feet in the air; a giant of a vegetable.

But it was not its size that now impressed my companions; it was the knowledge that seven hundred thousand pounds in gold lay somewhere buried beneath its spreading shadow.

Silver hobbled, grunting, on his crutch; and I read his thoughts like print. I could not doubt that he hoped to seize upon the treasure, find the *Hispaniola* under cover of night, cut every honest throat about that island, and sail away laden with crimes and riches.

We were now at the margin of the thicket.

"Huzza, mates, all together!" shouted Merry; and the foremost broke into a run.

And suddenly, not ten yards farther, we beheld them stop. A low cry arose.

Before us was a great excavation, not very recent, for grass had sprouted on the bottom. In this were the boards of several packing cases strewn around. On one of these boards I saw, branded with a hot iron, the name *Walrus*—the name of Flint's ship.

All was clear to probation. The cache had been found and rifled; the seven hundred thousand pounds were gone!

There was never such an overturn in this world. But Silver kept his head, and changed his plan before the others had had time to realise the disappointment.

He began moving quietly northward, and in a few steps had put the hollow between us two and the other five. I could not forbear whispering, "So you've changed sides again."

The buccaneers began to leap into the pit and to dig with their fingers. Morgan found a piece of gold.

"Two guineas!" he roared, shaking it at Silver. "That's your seven hundred thousand pounds, is it? You're him that never bungled nothing, you wooden-headed lubber!"

Well, there we stood, two on the one side, five on the other, the pit between us.

"Mates," says Merry, at last, "there's two of them alone there."

He was raising his arms and his voice, and plainly meant to lead a charge. But just then—*crack! crack! crack!*—three musket shots flashed out. Merry tumbled head foremost into the pit; another of the pirates fell; and the other three turned and ran for it with all their might.

The doctor, Gray, and Ben Gunn joined us, with smoking muskets, from among the nutmeg trees.

"Forward!" cried the doctor. "Double quick, my lads. We must head 'em off the boats."

And we set off, at a great pace.

When we reached the brow of the slope, we could see the three survivors running right for Mizzen-mast Hill. We were already between them and the boats; and so we four sat down to breathe, while Long John, mopping his face, came slowly up with us.

As we proceeded leisurely downhill to where the boats were lying, the doctor related what had taken place. Ben Gunn was the hero from beginning to end.

Ben, in his long, lonely wanderings about the island, had found the skeleton; he had found the treasure; had dug it up; and had carried it on his back, in many weary journeys, to his cave at the north-east angle of the island.

When the doctor had wormed this secret from him, on the afternoon of the attack, and when next morning he saw the anchorage deserted, he had gone to Silver, given him the chart, which was now useless, and moved in safety from the stockade to the two-pointed hill, there to keep a guard upon the money.

That morning, finding that I was to be involved in the horrid disappointment he had prepared for the mutineers, he had run all the way to the cave, had taken Gray and Ben Gunn, and started across the island, to be at hand beside the pine. Soon, however, he saw that our party had the start of him; and Ben Gunn, being fleet of foot, went ahead alone. Then it had occurred to him to work upon the superstitions of his former shipmates.

By this time we had reached the gigs. The doctor, with a pickaxe, demolished one of them, and then we all got aboard the other and set out for North Inlet.

Three miles out, what should we meet but the *Hispaniola*, cruising by herself! The last flood had lifted her, and there was little amiss, beyond the wreck of the mainsail. Another anchor was dropped in a fathom and a half of water. We all pulled into Rum Cove, where a gentle slope ran up to the cave. At the top, the squire met us.

"John Silver," he said, "you're a prodigious villain and impostor. I am told I am not to prosecute you. But the dead men, sir, hang about your neck like millstones."

The cave was a large, airy place, with a little spring and a pool of clear water, overhung with ferns. Before a big fire lay Captain Smollett: and in a far corner, only duskily flickered over by the blaze, I beheld great heaps of coin and bars of gold. That was Flint's treasure that we had come so far to seek, and that had cost already the lives of seventeen men from the *Hispaniola*.

What a supper I had of it that night, with all my friends around me; and what a meal it was, with Benn Gunn's salted goat, and some delicacies and a bottle of old wine from the *Hispaniola*!

The next morning we fell early to work, and Gray and Ben Gunn came and went with the boat, while the rest piled treasure on the beach.

It was a strange collection. English, French, Spanish, Portugese, Georges, and Louises, doubloons and double guineas and moidores and sequins—nearly every variety of money in the world must, I think, have found a place in that collection.

Silver, I should say, was allowed his entire liberty, yet none treated him better than a dog; except Ben Gunn, who was still terribly afraid of his old quartermaster.

"I'm on your side now, hand and glove," said Silver.

"Well," said the doctor, "you're the man to keep your word, we know that."

A council was held, and it was decided that we must desert the three pirates on the island. We left a good stock of powder and shot, the bulk of the salt goat, and some other necessaries. And at last, one fine morning, we weighed anchor, and stood out of North Inlet.

The three fellows must have been watching us closer than we thought, for, coming through the narrows, we saw all three of them kneeling together on a spit of sand, with their arms raised in supplication. It went to all our hearts to leave them in that wretched state; but to take them home for the gibbet would have been a cruel sort of kindness.

The spit itself had soon melted out of sight; and before noon, to my inexpressible joy, the highest rock of Treasure Island had sunk into the blue round of sea.

We laid her head for the nearest port in Spanish America, to engage fresh hands.

It was just at sundown when we cast anchor in a most beautiful land-locked gulf. The lights that began to shine in the town made a most charming contrast to our dark and bloody sojourn on the island; and the doctor and the squire, taking me along with them, went ashore to pass the night.

Next day, as soon as we came on the *Hispaniola*, Ben Gunn began to make us a confession. Silver was gone. Gunn had connived at his escape in a shore boat, and he now assured us he had only done so to preserve our lives. But the sea-cook had not gone empty-handed. Unobserved, he had removed one of the sacks of coin, worth three or four hundred guineas.

I think we were all pleased to be so cheaply quit of him.

Well, to make a long story short, we got a few hands on board, and made a good cruise home.

All of us had an ample share of the treasure, and used it wisely or foolishly, according to our natures. Captain Smollett is now retired from the sea. As for Ben Gunn, he got a thousand pounds, which he spent or lost in three weeks. Then he was given a lodge to keep; and he still lives, a great favourite with the country boys, and a notable singer in church on Sundays and saints' days.

Of Silver we have heard no more. That formidable seafaring man with one leg has at last gone clean out of my life; but I dare say he met his wife, and perhaps still lives in comfort with her and Captain Flint.

Oxen and wain-ropes would not bring me back again to that accursed island; and the worst dreams that ever I have are when I hear the surf booming about its coasts, or start upright in bed, with the sharp voice of Captain Flint still ringing in my ears: "Pieces of eight! pieces of eight!"